NEVER Teach a STEGOSAURUS to do Sums

For Ishaan and Anaya, who love numbers
as much as they love words. x
R.S.

For SBE. I wish you could see this
D.E.

PUFFIN BOOKS
UK | USA | Canada | Ireland | Australia | India | New Zealand | South Africa
Puffin Books is part of the Penguin Random House group of companies
whose addresses can be found at global.penguinrandomhouse.com.

First published 2021
001

Printed and bound in China
ISBN: 978-0-241-38743-6

The authorized representative in the EEA is Penguin Random House Ireland,
Morrison Chambers, 32 Nassau Street, Dublin D02 YH68

A CIP catalogue record for this book is available from the British Library

All correspondence to: Puffin Books, Penguin Random House Children's
One Embassy Gardens, New Union Square, 5 Nine Elms Lane, London SW8 5DA

NEVER Teach a STEGOSAURUS to do Sums

Rashmi Sirdeshpande & Diane Ewen

PUFFIN

NEVER

teach a **Stegosaurus**

to do sums.

Because if you do . . .

. . . there's no end to what she might do with all those numbers.

Like **adding** them up,

taking them away

and a few other sneaky tricks too!

And if she masters all those, she'll be having **SO much** fun that she won't want to stop!

Just you wait until she figures out how she can **USE** all those numbers and sums to crack codes . . .

bake things . . .

build things . . .

and make things
do stuff!

Who knew numbers
could do all this?

And once she figures THAT out,
what do you think she'll set her sights on next?

Ahhhh, yes . . .

She'll want to make herself a rocket
to go to the moon, Mars
and BEYOND.

Obviously.

STEP 1 - THE MOON
SPACE KIT
R

Of course, she won't be able to do it alone.

SO, while she's in the mood
for all that making

and coding,

she'll build a few helpers first.
Like THESE ones
right here.

That's better.

And with their help . . .
and a bit of tugging
and tapping
and tinkering . . .
Dino-Lux
Spaceship paint
STEP 1 – THE MOON
. . . it will FINALLY be ready.

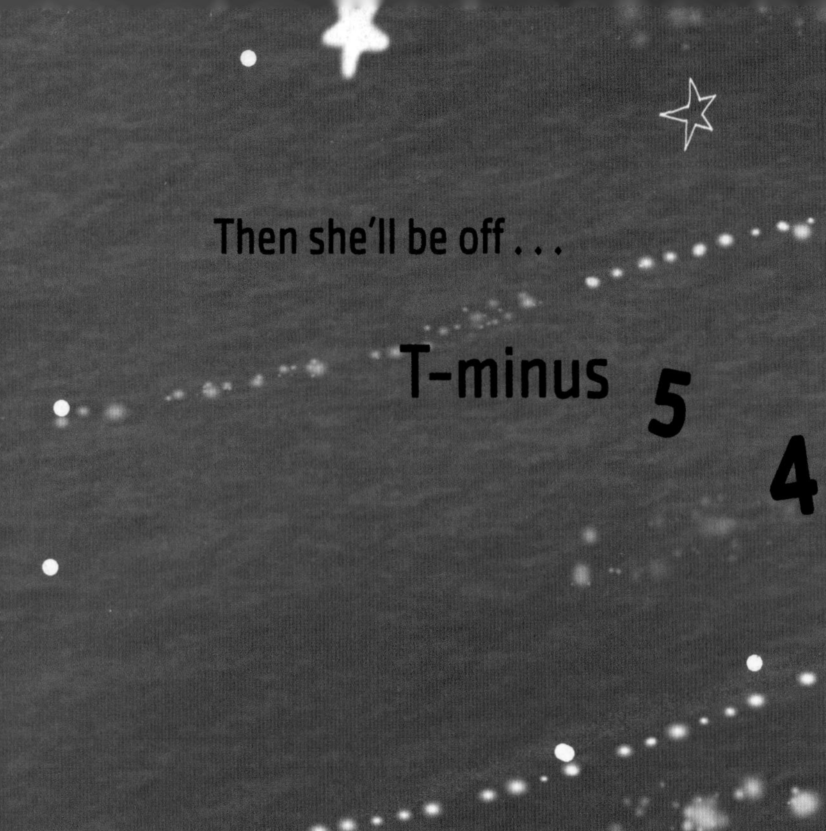

Then she'll be off . . .

T-minus 5 4 3 2 1

STEG 'O' SOAR
ANNNNNND . . .

NOTHING.

OOPS.

That's OK. If at first she doesn't succeed, she'll try again.

And again . . .

AND AGAIN . . .

Until she finally cracks it!

And if she makes it into space . . .

. . . she's BOUND to make
some out-of-this-world friends
while she's up there.

She might even find they've got LOTS in common!

Because maybe . . .

just maybe . . .

aliens **LOVE** numbers –

AND ROBOTS –

too!

But she can't stay there forever

and at some point she'll have to go back home.

So there will be some very teary goodbyes . . .

And if she comes back from outer space . . .

. . . she'll definitely bring some bright ideas with her!

But if she makes those robots . . .

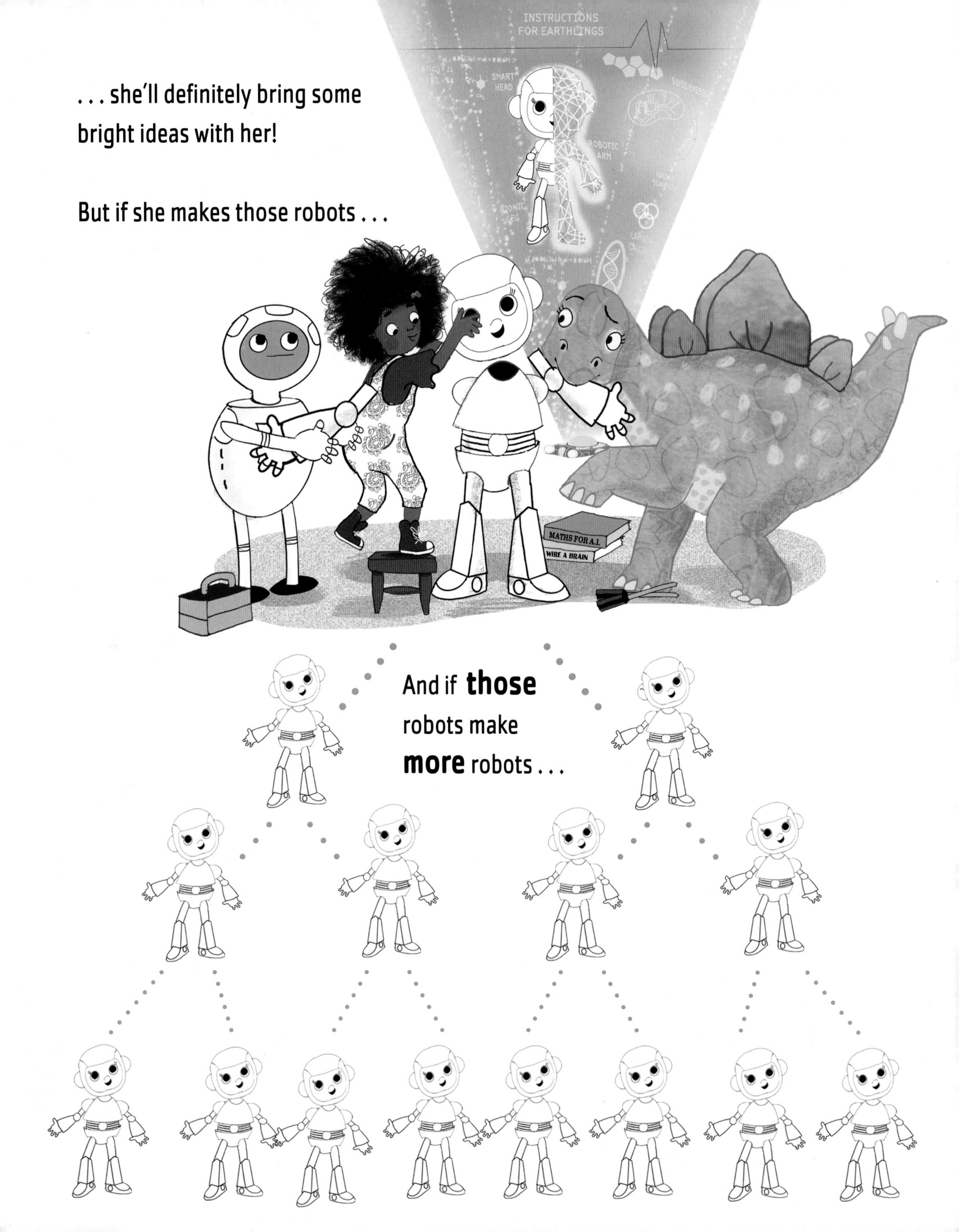

And if **those** robots make **more** robots . . .

And THOSE
robots make
WorkerBot
ChefBot
NannyBot
HOW TO WIRE A BRAIN
EVEN
MORE
robots . . .

Well, **then** they'll be
EVERYWHERE
The Three Little Robots

and things might just get
a **TEENSY** bit out of control . . .

And if THAT happens, we're really going to need Steggy to pull something out of the bag.

Because . . .

Hang on . . .

What's that, Steggy?

You're absolutely right!

That's why you **always** make an **OFF** button! PHEW.
OFF

And if Steggy presses that OFF button and manages to sort out
all that mess, what do you suppose she'll want to do NEXT???

You know what?
It's been a long day, so she'll probably
want to snuggle up
and **count** the stars
in the night sky . . .

KATHERINE
JOHNSON
Mathematician and
human computer at NASA!
NASA
98
99
100
z z z
z
NEVER
Show
a
T-REX
a
Book

Besides, it's ALWAYS a good idea

to save a BIT of fun for tomorrow . . .